"...my favourite book of the year – in which Lionel
the cat reveals what he does when his mistress is out –
all illustrated by Ingman's fantastic...paintings."
HARPERS & QUEEN

"Oversized and irresistable...
it will inspire laughs out loud from all readers,
no matter what their ages."
Kirkus Reviews

"...this book is both a dazzling debut, and a tour de force."
Ian Beck, Mother Goose Judging Panel

ALBERT

Audrey

Flash Harry

Martha

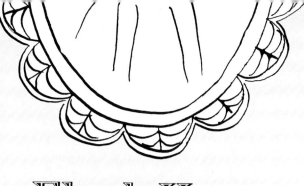

Gladys

Martha

ALBERT

WHEN THE

THE MICE

LIONEL

MARTHA'S

CATS AWAY

WILL PLAY

When you go off to school,
you think I just sleep all day:
WELL, BOY,
HAVE I GOT NEWS
FOR YOU!

I have my own newspaper delivered to keep myself up-to-date with the goings-on in the cat world.

I keep myself fit to make sure that the dog next door can't catch me.

At ten o'clock I set up my easel and paints and *Gladys* from No. 34 pops round to pose for me.

I cook myself a spot of lunch: my favourite is a nice bit of salmon washed down with a cool saucer of milk.

I like to watch the cartoons
while I have my lunch.

I phone my cousin **ALBERT** in Skegness for a chat.

Sometimes in the afternoon Flash Harry knocks on the back door with his suitcase full of goodies.

I have a little nap and, WOW,
do I have some good dreams.

I listen to the radio. I like the gardening programmes that tell me all about the plants and flowers in our garden.

Then I go upstairs to get changed for my afternoon performance.

Cats come from far and near
to hear me play.

They are very
generous with their
applause and I usually
do a couple of encores.

I play with your toys. *Audrey* from
across the road calls round quite often
to play doctors and nurses.

If there's any time to spare, I take the car
for a quick spin around your room.

When I hear the garden gate, I dash downstairs to the sofa and pretend to be in the Land of Nod. Then you rush into the room and kiss me hello, thinking I have been asleep all day.

Well, now you know!

This book
is especially
for Jessie

ALBERT

Audrey

Flash Harry

Martha

Flash Harry

Gladys

Martha

ALBERT

First published in Great Britain 1995
by Methuen Children's Books
Published 1996 by Mammoth
an imprint of Reed Consumer Books Ltd
Michelin House, 81 Fulham Road, London SW3 6RB
and Auckland, Melbourne, Singapore and Toronto
10 8 6 4 2 1 3 5 7 9

ISBN 0 7497 2957 0

A CIP catalogue record for this book
is available from the British Library

Produced by Mandarin Offset Ltd
Printed and bound in China

Typeset by Bruce Ingman, Genevieve Webster
and Alan Kitching at the Typography Workshop
London